God

Interpreter of the Dragon

By John J Wiseley

Table of Contents

Whisper of Flames.........................5
Lessons of Fire and Spirit...............9
A New Warrior............................16
An Apt Pupil.............................22
The Reckoning............................30
The Cave.................................39
The Meeting..............................43
The Great Fall...........................48
A Call to Arms...........................52
The War Fleet............................56
The Brothers' Felspar....................61
The Fated Duo............................66

GODWULF

WHISPER OF FLAMES

The morning mist clung to the rolling hills of the English countryside, a soft shroud that concealed the world beneath its weight. Sunlight struggled through the silvery veil, casting a gentle glow over the lush pastures where grazing sheep bobbed their heads like soft clouds on the ground. Among these quiet slopes and fields, the air was alive with the chorus of nature, birds sang melodies while the brook gurgled cheerfully in its winding path.

Osric, a sturdy sheepherder with a sun-weathered face, stood at the edge of his flock. His hands, calloused yet gentle, cradled a small lamb, while his heart swelled with pride at his two sons, Godwulf and Leofric, as they chased each other, laughter spilling forth like the sweet nectar of blooming heather.

Godwulf, the elder, carried an air of spirited determination, his eyes sharp and astute. Leofric, youthful and innocent, followed with boundless enthusiasm, embodying the very essence of joy, oblivious to the lurking shadows beyond their pastoral life.

The sun climbed higher, casting away the fog, and the

horizon shimmered with unspoken promises of the day ahead. But as laughter filled the air, a darker note tremored beneath the surface, unheard by those who dwelled in the simplicity of their lives. Whispers of fate lingered, ready to unfold their grim tapestry.

As the sun reached its zenith, the tranquility shattered. The thunderous clang of iron met the stillness as the ground vibrated beneath the marauding hooves of Norikai warriors. Their fierce longships had carved a passage through the waters, driven by the bloodlust of their chieftain, Farfel. The Viking clan, notorious for their brutality, descended upon the unsuspecting village like an oncoming storm, sweeping through homes and fields with an insatiable hunger for chaos.

Osric stood frozen, an iron weight forming in his chest as he reached for his sons, his calloused hands shaking. The chaos erupted around him, the fires blazed, smoke roiled into the sky, and the cries of the villagers mingled with the clangor of swords. Godwulf and Leofric clung to his side, eyes wide as the invasion unfurled before them, the innocence of their youth shattered.

"Stay close!"

Osric commanded, his voice hoarse as he shielded his sons from the frenzy.

But retreat could not be found. Norikai warriors swarmed like a horde of shadows, separating families and snatching the children from the safety of their homes. In a horrifying moment, Farfel appeared, his countenance twisted with madness, his eyes alight as he scanned the field for potential prey.

Osric fought against the tide of panic, gripping Godwulf's arm tightly, but it was Leofric who cried out.

"Father!" he pleaded, trying to break free from the grasp that kept him tethered.

Before Osric could respond, a Norikai warrior lunged forward, seizing Leofric and dragging him away, the child's screams swallowed by the roaring flames and the menacing laughter of their captors.

"Leofric!" Godwulf shouted, his voice an echo of desperation as he lunged forward.

He clawed at the air, trying to grasp the hem of his brother's tunic. But it was too late; Leofric was swept into the chaos, his cries fading into sorrowful whispers.

As the village burned, Osric crumpled to his knees, the weight of despair shattering his resolve.

Godwulf's spirit burned with fury as he helped his father to stand, igniting a fire in his heart. They had to act; they could not let darkness steal his brother's light.

Days passed since the raid, time marked only by the ashes of their home and the shadows that danced in the corner of Osric's mind. The village no longer hummed with life, and the once-vibrant fields lay desolate. Determined to reclaim his son, Osric gathered his breath and sought help where the village's last remnants of hope remained, in the monastery perched upon the hill.

With heavy hearts, a weakened resolve, and visions of their lost Leofric haunting their thoughts, father and son climbed the path to the ancient stone walls. The monks, keepers of knowledge and guardians of wisdom, welcomed them with solemn expressions. They exchanged glances, sensing the unspoken tragedy that had befallen Osric's family.

"We must train him in the ways of the dragon," the abbot spoke, his voice a deep rumble that echoed in the stone chamber.

"Only the strength of the dragon can face such evil."

Godwulf felt the churn of something within him, an awakening that reached into his soul, igniting a flicker of hope amidst the despair. The dragons of legend, not mere creatures of fire and flight, but symbols of power and protection.

JOHN J WISELEY

LESSONS OF FIRE AND SPIRIT

The first light of dawn spread a golden hue over the monastery of Lindisfarne, where stone walls stood resolute against the tempest of fate. Godwulf rose with the sun, his heart heavy with grief but resolute in purpose. Each morning was marked by the same ritual, awakening in the austere bedding provided by the monks, his mind consumed by the image of his younger brother and the fires that had consumed their village.

As the day unfurled, Godwulf joined the other initiates of the monastery, a gathering of young souls seeking wisdom and strength. Among them was Komo, a monk whose presence was commanding yet gentle, with a light in his eyes that spoke of ancient knowledge and a deep connection to the ethereal. He was an unusual figure, wrapped in the simple robes of the brethren, yet his bearing inspired reverence. Komo was often spoken of in hushed tones, the one chosen to guide Godwulf in the ways of the dragon.

"Come, Godwulf," Komo beckoned, motioning to a secluded grove where sunlight filtered softly through the leaves.

"Today, we begin your true training."

Anxiety knotted in Godwulf's stomach as he followed the monk, the scent of earth and flowers wafting around them. He had heard tales of the rigorous exercises and disciplines that lay ahead, and while anticipation coursed through him, doubts flickered at the edges of his mind.

"Sit," Komo instructed, gesturing to a flat stone.

Godwulf obeyed, crossing his legs beneath him and adopting a stance of calm.

"Close your eyes and take a breath. Let the world fade."

Compelled by the warmth of Komo's voice, Godwulf drew in a steadying breath. The sounds of the forest receded. With every inhale, he felt the weight of the past dissipate, and with each exhale, he released his sorrows.

They stirred like leaves in the wind but drifted farther away into the expanse of quiet.

"Now, focus your will," Komo continued, his tone melodic and resonant.

"Picture the essence of the dragon, mighty, wise, and eternal."

Godwulf envisioned the dragon, its scales glimmering under a sun that never set, beating its powerful wings against the heavens. A warmth bloomed in his chest; he could almost feel its presence wrapping around him like a protective mantle.

"Good," Komo whispered, lifting his hands in a graceful motion, urging Godwulf deeper into his concentration.

"You are ready to journey beyond this realm. With your spirit, you will enter the ethereal library, a sanctuary of ancient wisdom, where scrolls whisper the secrets of our kind."

As Komo's words unfurled in the air, shimmering light enveloped Godwulf, spiraling and swirling like the winds of an unseen cyclone.

His breath quickened, and he felt heavier, grounded yet set adrift. The forest around him fell away, and in a blink, he was no longer seated upon the stone.

He stood in a vast expanse filled with colors and sounds beyond comprehension, each hue resonating with the essence of a world unseen. Before him loomed an immense library, constructed of amber light and the shimmering dust of forgotten ages. Ancient scrolls floated amid the air, each one infused with the knowledge of countless generations. Their presence beckoned him forth, calling like distant stars in the night sky.

"Welcome, Godwulf," echoed a voice within him, familiar yet ethereal.

"You have entered the sacred domain of the dragon's counsel."

With a leap of understanding, Godwulf reached for the nearest scroll. Its surface felt warm beneath his fingertips, and as he unrolled it, symbols and illustrations danced along the length of its parchment. Each secret of the dragon, its wisdom, its power, unfurled before his eyes, enriching his spirit.

He gleaned lessons on strength coupled with compassion, tactics tempered with ethics, and the bond between dragon and warrior, a symbiosis forged in the fires of unity.

Time slipped from his grasp as Godwulf immersed himself

within the knowledge, absorbing the teachings as they resonated with his very soul.

Yet, amidst the quiet whispers of scrolls, a pang of desperation broke through his focus, Leofric. Images of his brother plagued him, urging him to remember his purpose.

In an instant, the ethereal library faded, and he was propelled through layers of existence, hurtling toward reality like a fractured fragment of a dream. Godwulf gasped, returning to the serene grove where Komo awaited.

"Welcome back," Komo said, a knowing smile gracing his lips.

"Tell me, what did you learn?"

"Everything—" Godwulf stammered, breathless.

"The power of the dragon, the bond it holds with its warrior. I saw... my brother's face. I cannot

Komo's gaze intensified, locking onto Godwulf with a weight that bore down on the young man's mind.

"You believe you've learned everything," he said, his voice calm yet firm, "but this is merely the beginning. The true path of the dragon is deeper than the scrolls and teachings you've touched. It lies in understanding the language of the dragon, the most sacred and powerful of arts."

Godwulf blinked, confusion rippling through him.

"The language of the dragon?" he echoed, a thread of uncertainty entering his tone.

"What do you mean?"

"It is a telepathic language," Komo explained, his expression serious.

"A language that flows between thoughts and emotions, a connection deeper than mere words. Those who can wield it do not simply speak; they commune. The risks, however, are profound.

The power contained within can heal or destroy, it can call forth dragons or extinguish the lives of men. Used incorrectly, it could spell chaos rather than harmony."

He paused, the air thickening with a sense of gravity.

"The last known interpreter of this language died many seasons ago, leaving the dragon clans fractured and leaderless. Since that time, messages between the clans have faltered; without their ability to communicate, they have descended into strife. The balance of our world has crumbled, and darkness has taken root."

Godwulf felt a chill run along his spine, the implications of Komo's words settling into the corners of his mind.

"And the Draco Supreme?" he asked, desperate to understand.

"Where can we find him?"

Komo's expression darkened, shadows flickering across his brows.

"Alas, his whereabouts remain a mystery. Many believe he is still alive, wandering the hidden realms, waiting for the next worthy interpreter to find him. Without the Draco Supreme, the essence of the dragon remains in disarray, and our task is to seek him before the balance shatters completely."

"But how?" Godwulf pressed, determination igniting anew within him.

The quest to find Leofric surged through him, intertwining with a newfound call to restore peace.

"If the scrolls have shown me the bond with the dragons, then surely I can seek this interpreter as well."

Komo rested a hand on Godwulf's shoulder, steadying him.

"Patience, Godwulf. This journey will require more than mere will. You will need to delve deeper into your understanding of the dragon's spirit, there beneath your anger lies clarity, but you must first learn the language. Only then can you hope to navigate the realms and renew the harmony we so desperately seek."

The thought of such a great task loomed before Godwulf, transforming the trepidation within him to a burning aspiration. An ember of hope glowed brightly; he could do this, and he would do this, not just for Leofric, but for the very fabric of their world.

"I promise I will learn," Godwulf affirmed, biting off each word with unwavering conviction.

"Teach me what I must know to find the Draco Supreme, and I will be ready."

"In time, we shall prepare you," Komo responded, a faint smile breaking the somber weight of the moment.

"The path you tread is long and fraught with trials, but it begins with mastering the energy that flows through you. Meet me at the grove each day. We will redefine your connection with the spirit of the dragon until you can reach him and understand his will."

As the days turned into weeks, Godwulf devoted himself to the training, each lesson driven by a singular intent.

He learned the meditation practices required to calm his restless spirit, honing the impulses of his heart and mind until they resided in perfect harmony. Under Komo's guidance, each attempt to connect with the essence of dragons drew him into deeper knowledge. He began to hear whispers, not words spoken aloud, but vibrations of understanding that wrapped around him like a caress.

"Focus on feeling," Komo urged as they sat together near a stream, the gentle water another voice in the symphony of nature.

"Let the energy of the world around you connect with your

heart's pulse. Dragons embody an ancient wisdom; they speak in feels and desires, not just commands."

Godwulf cultivated this connection, struggling yet persevering, as existential threads of insight wove themselves into his understanding like golden threads in a tapestry. But every time he reached for the ethereal connection, he faced barriers, shadows of doubt or bursts of fear that clouded his mind. It was as if a ferocious tempest lurked just beyond the tranquility he sought.

"Do not fear the tempest," Komo reminded him one evening, the setting sun bathing the sky in hues of crimson and gold.

"Embrace it. The fury of storms is nothing compared to the power it can unleash. Control it, and you learn the language of the dragon."

"Control…" Godwulf whispered, a hint of realization.

A NEW WARRIOR

Leofric gasped as the thick wooden staff cracked across his ribs, sending him sprawling into the cold, wet mud. Pain shot through his side, and he struggled to pull air into his lungs. Above him, the towering figure of Farfel sneered, his scarred face twisted with cruel amusement.

"Get up, thrall," Farfel growled.

"A warrior does not rest on his back like a woman."

Leofric pushed himself onto his hands and knees, spitting blood into the dirt. His body was riddled with bruises from days of relentless training, and his muscles ached from exhaustion. Yet, he knew there was no mercy to be found in this place. Not among these men. Not among the Northmen.

The Viking horde was vast, three thousand strong and ever-growing, their numbers swelled by the captured and the willing alike. They sailed the seas in thirty great longships, swift and deadly, their hulls slicing through the waves like a wolf pack on the hunt. Slaves were their currency, their way of life. They raided with a singular purpose: to take what they could and destroy what they could not.

Beyond the raids, their homeland was a land of ice and fire, fjords cutting deep into the land, ring forts dotting the coasts like the bones of giants. These forts, built of thick wooden palisades and deep trenches, served as both protection and places of trade. Here, warriors trained, feasted, and prepared for war, while the captured were broken and reforged into either slaves or warriors.

And Leofric was to become one of them.

Farfel circled him like a predator playing with its wounded prey.

"You will learn, Saxon," he said, driving his boot into Leofric's ribs, rolling him onto his back.

"Or you will die."

Leofric had lost count of the beatings. Every morning, he was dragged from the wooden hut where he and the other captives slept, fed only enough to keep him moving. Then, the training began.

They made him fight, first with wooden weapons, then with dulled steel. They beat him when he faltered, struck him down when he hesitated. The weak were weeded out. Those who could not keep up were cast aside, left to rot or be sold like cattle.

The Northmen knew how to strip a man of his past. They deprived him of warmth, of comfort, of familiarity. They spoke to him only in their own tongue, forcing him to learn their words or suffer for his ignorance. At night, they filled his ears with stories of their gods, Odin, the Allfather, who demanded sacrifice and strength; Thor, the god of thunder, whose hammer crushed his foes; Loki, the trickster, who played with fate like a child's toy.

"The gods have willed this," Farfel told him one night, after yet another brutal sparring session.

"You were born to be weak, but we will make you strong. We will carve the cowardice from your bones."

Leofric lay in the straw, his body too battered to move. He wanted to resist, to cling to the fire that had burned in his heart when he had first been taken. But the truth was undeniable.

Every day, he became less of who he had been. Every day, he fought harder, endured more. And every day, he feared he was beginning to believe them.

Leofric awoke to the familiar bite of the cold, his breath a pale mist in the dim morning light.

The air was thick with the scent of damp straw and unwashed bodies, but today, something was different. Farfel's heavy bootsteps did not echo through the longhouse. Instead, a new figure loomed over him, a man with olive skin, dark hair, and sharp, calculating eyes.

"Get up, Saxon," the man said, his voice laced with an accent Leofric did not recognize.

"I am your new master of arms. You will call me Rodrigo."

Leofric hesitated only for a moment before rising. He had learned long ago that hesitation led to pain. But Rodrigo did not strike him, nor did he sneer as Farfel had. The Spaniard simply studied him, his gaze appraising.

"Farfel would break you before he made you strong," Rodrigo said, leading Leofric outside.

The cold wind sliced through Leofric's thin tunic, but he no longer flinched at its touch.

"But a man who is broken is unpredictable. You understand why I treat you differently?"

Leofric did not answer at first. Finally, he muttered,

"You do not want me to kill you when I am strong."

Rodrigo smiled, a flicker of amusement crossing his weathered face.

"Exactly. You are learning."

The training was different under Rodrigo. He did not beat Leofric for failing, though failure was still met with punishment, it was calculated, meant to correct rather than destroy. He taught Leofric to read an opponent's movements, to strike not with blind rage but with intent. The sword was an extension of the arm, the shield a moving fortress. Under Rodrigo's guidance, Leofric's bruises began to fade, replaced with hardened muscle and sharpened skill.

The long, cold seasons of Norway stretched endlessly. The sun barely graced the sky during winter, and when it did, it was weak, casting only a pale glow before retreating again. The men gathered around fires at night, drinking and speaking of raids to come, of warm lands across the sea where the sun never hid and the soil was rich. Rodrigo spoke of such places, of his home in Al-Andalus, where the air was thick with the scent of oranges and the seas were warm as bathwater.

Leofric listened, though he had never known warmth outside the forge of battle.

"You will be strong," Rodrigo told him one evening as they stood beneath the snow-laden sky, the training yard empty but for the two of them.

"Stronger than Farfel ever imagined. And when that day comes, remember who gave you the means to be more than a thrall."

Leofric met Rodrigo's gaze. The Spaniard was no friend, he

was still a captor, still a man who held power over him. But in a world of cruelty, Rodrigo was the closest thing to an ally he had.

Leofric grew stronger with each passing raid. He had started as a mere boy, but now, as the Northmen swept through villages and fortresses alike, his name was whispered with both fear and admiration. He fought fiercely, wielding his sword with a skill that surpassed many of his so-called masters. His arms thickened, his frame broadened, and his presence on the battlefield became impossible to ignore.

With every victory, Leofric felt the chains of his past loosening. The men he once served as a slave now called him brother in war.

Rodrigo watched his progress closely, often giving him advice in hushed tones before the next battle.

"Strike with purpose. Do not waste movement. Every breath counts."

Farfel, who had once taken pleasure in beating him, now began to take notice. The glances were subtle at first, a narrowed eye, a lingering gaze during feasts. But soon, they became more than that. Leofric could feel the weight of Farfel's scrutiny, the way the seasoned warrior measured him now not as a slave, but as a potential threat.

During one particularly brutal raid, Leofric had taken down three men in quick succession, his blade moving as if guided by the gods. As the village burned behind them, Farfel approached, his expression unreadable.

"You fight well," he admitted, his voice lacking its usual mockery.

"Perhaps too well."

Leofric met his gaze without flinching. He was no longer the beaten thrall crawling in the dirt. He was something else now, something stronger. And Farfel knew it.

THE APT PUPIL

Komo decided that it was time to move Godwulf to the next step. The cave of the dead was half a day's journey. The trip was long and arduous, the wheels of the cart groaning under the weight of supplies as Komo guided the horse through the winding, frost-laden path. Godwulf sat in silence, wrapped in thick furs, his breath forming misty clouds in the frigid air. The dense forest around them stretched endlessly, the towering pines casting long shadows as the sun began its slow descent behind the mountains.

Komo had spoken little since they departed from the monastery. It was only after several hours that he finally broke the silence.

"You have learned much, Godwulf. But what you seek now requires solitude. Discipline. The Draco Supreme will not grant his presence lightly, nor will Hycrest entertain a mind unprepared."

Godwulf nodded, gripping the hilt of his blade.

"I understand."

"Do you?" Komo glanced at him, his piercing eyes unreadable.

"You have trained your body, but your mind still clings to

distractions. In this cave, you will be alone with your thoughts. You will meditate, listen to the wind, and speak to the unseen. If the Draco Supreme deems you worthy, he will answer."

The cart rumbled on through the narrowing mountain pass, the snow thickening around them. Hours passed before they arrived at the cave, a massive, yawning maw in the side of the mountain, its depths obscured by darkness. The air was thick with the scent of damp stone and ancient mystery.

Komo dismounted first, gesturing for Godwulf to follow.

"This will be your home for as long as it takes. There is food and water within, but they will not last forever. You must learn to sustain yourself with what the land provides. No fire, no comfort, only focus."

Godwulf stepped forward, peering into the cave. He could feel the weight of it, the history buried in its cold, jagged walls. He inhaled deeply, steadying himself.

"And if I fail?"

Komo's expression did not change.

"Then you were never meant to walk this path."

Without another word, Komo turned back to the cart, preparing to leave. Godwulf watched him, knowing that when the sound of hooves faded into the wind, he would be utterly alone.

Steeling himself, he took his first steps into the darkness, ready to seek the voice of the Draco Supreme.

The first few days were grueling. Godwulf adapted slowly, making the cave his home as best he could. He found furs to sleep in, remnants of old hunts left behind by some past dweller. He gathered what little food he could, catching fish from a narrow stream that cut through the rocks, trapping small animals when the opportunity arose. The days were long and silent, save for the whispering wind that echoed through the cavern. At night, the cold crept in, but he endured it, as Komo had instructed.

Each day, he meditated. He sat cross-legged upon the cold stone, focusing his thoughts, clearing his mind. At first, it was nothing but frustration, his thoughts drifted, memories clawed at him, the emptiness of solitude pressing in like a great weight.

But he persisted. He listened to the wind, to the distant howls of wolves, to the slow drip of water against stone.

Then, on the seventh day, something changed.

As he sat in deep meditation, his mind drifted beyond the cave, beyond the mountain. A great warmth filled his chest, an energy unlike anything he had felt before. Then, a voice, deep, ancient, resonating like the rumbling of a thousand storms.

"Godwulf. You seek knowledge."

His eyes snapped open, yet he was not in the cave. He was floating in an expanse of golden light, his body weightless, his breath stolen from him. And before him, emerging from the void, was a presence so immense it defied comprehension, a dragon, its scales shimmering with hues of silver and gold, its eyes like molten fire.

"Draco Supreme..." Godwulf whispered, his voice barely more than a breath.

"You have endured, and thus you are granted my voice."

The great dragon's wings spread wide, casting shadows that rippled through the golden void.

"Know this, mortal. You walk the path of the dragons,

but you are not yet among them. To stand with us, you must understand us."

The light around them shifted, revealing a vision of dragons soaring through the skies, each unique, their forms displaying colors that danced like gemstones in the sun.

"There are six great clans," Draco Supreme continued.

"Obsidian, the guardians of the depths, forged in fire and stone. Amethyst, the protectors of my sacred domain, swift and wise beyond time. Sapphire, the seekers of knowledge, their wisdom rivaled only by their cunning. Hydrous, the rulers of the tides, the bridge between land and sea. Citrine, the wanderers, ever moving, ever adapting. And Varaquiose, the stormcallers, whose wrath shakes the heavens."

Godwulf watched in awe as the dragons circled above him, their roars shaking the very fabric of the vision.

"There are only twenty-two of us left. Twenty-two dragons still walk this world, aside from myself. And each one is bound to their purpose. You must find yours."

The light began to fade, and with it, the great presence of Draco Supreme.

"Seek Hycrest. He will know if you are worthy. But beware, mortal, there are those who would see the dragons fall. If you are to stand among us, you must be ready to fight."

Then, darkness.

Godwulf gasped as he awoke, his body drenched in sweat despite the frigid air. He sat up, his heart pounding, his mind reeling from what he had just experienced. The path was now clear. He had been given the first step. He would seek Hycrest, and he would prove his worth.

Determined to prepare himself for the journey ahead, Godwulf deepened his meditation. He spent days refining his connection to the unseen energies around him, feeling the pulse of the land, the whispers of the wind. He honed his survival skills, learning to track larger prey, craft simple tools, and anticipate the shifts in the weather. The solitude that once weighed heavy upon him now felt like an ally, sharpening his focus and discipline.

A week passed, then another. His body grew leaner, harder, honed by the rigors of living off the land. His mind became sharper, more attuned to the world beyond sight.

As the cold wind howled across the mountains, Godwulf sat in the cave, his breath coming out in visible clouds. He had spent days in isolation, reflecting, meditating, and practicing his contact rituals under Komo's guidance.

The deep silence of the cave was unlike any he had experienced before, but it wasn't discomfort that gnawed at him, it was the anticipation of what was to come.

The Draco Supreme had allowed him this time to prepare, but now, he felt the connection coming closer. His thoughts focused on Hycrest, the leader of Clan Amethyst, the eldest of the dragons. Hycrest had known the ways of the ancient dragons and had long since attained the wisdom of ages. The stories about him were whispered in awe: his scales shimmered with an ethereal glow, his voice was like the rumble of thunder, and his wings, though rarely seen, could cast shadows over vast lands.

The air thickened, a low hum vibrating through the cave walls. Godwulf closed his eyes, his heartbeat steadying as he recalled the teachings of Komo. The ritual was simple in concept, yet difficult in execution, he had to clear his mind of distractions, focus solely on the connection to Hycrest, and trust in his abilities.

Minutes turned into hours, the darkness of the cave enveloping him completely, until, suddenly, it was as if the very air crackled. He felt the immense presence before he saw it. The temperature dropped sharply, and Godwulf opened his eyes to find a pair of glowing amber orbs staring at him from the shadowed corner of the cave.

A low, resonant voice filled the space.

"Godwulf. You have come a long way."

Godwulf's heart raced, but he stood his ground. The being before him was not a mere man, nor even a simple creature. It was Hycrest, in all his magnificence. His massive form remained cloaked in shadow, but Godwulf could see the outline of great wings folded tightly against his sides and the gleaming edges of his scales that reflected the faintest light.

"I have," Godwulf said, his voice steady.

"I have come to learn."

Hycrest let out a sound that was part rumble, part chuckle, the reverberation shaking the cave slightly.

"Learning is a lifelong pursuit. You are not yet ready to understand everything I know. But you will learn what I can teach."

With a swift movement, the dragon stepped forward, his presence overwhelming.

"Draco Supreme spoke of you with great respect. You are a warrior, but also a seeker of knowledge. You understand that true power is not only in the strength of the body but in the mind, the soul. Do you know why you were chosen?"

Godwulf swallowed hard but met the dragon's gaze.

"I believe it is because of my desire to protect and to understand. My clan's strength is my strength, but my mind… my mind seeks something deeper."

Hycrest nodded, his gaze piercing.

"You are wise for your years. But the journey ahead will not be easy. Clan Amethyst is bound to the Draco Supreme, and your bond to us will grow, but it will demand much from you.

Your connection to the dragons will alter your very being, Godwulf. Are you prepared for that?"

Godwulf paused, feeling the weight of Hycrest's words.

"I am," he said, conviction rising in his chest.

Hycrest seemed to consider him for a long moment before giving a slow, approving nod.

"Then it begins, Godwulf. You will follow the path of the dragons. From this moment on, you will be bound to Clan Amethyst."

The dragon's form began to shift, his body elongating and wings unfurling to their full span. A blinding flash of light engulfed the cave, and Godwulf was momentarily blinded by the brilliance of the dragon's transformation.

When the light dimmed, Hycrest stood before him in his true form, magnificent, towering, and impossibly ancient. His wings stretched wide, casting enormous shadows against the cave walls, and his breath exhaled in deep, rumbling gusts.

"Welcome to the clan, Godwulf," Hycrest said, his voice a deep, rumbling thunder that shook Godwulf's core.

"Now, let us see if you are worthy of the knowledge that lies within the heart of a dragon."

THE RECKONING

The biting cold of the Norwegian winter gnawed at Leofric's bones as he followed the orders of his captor, Farfel. Days blurred into nights as the relentless training continued under the harshest conditions. But now, things had begun to shift. Farfel's grip on Leofric had loosened ever so slightly, replaced by the presence of a new figure, one whose methods were different from the brutal ways of his Viking captor.

The Spaniard studied Leofric with more care than Farfel ever had. The training remained grueling, but there was a softness in Rodrigo's approach, a desire to teach rather than to punish.

Farfel would often stand off to the side, watching with his arms crossed, a scowl on his face. But there was nothing he could do. Rodrigo had earned the begrudging respect of the other Vikings with his sword skills and cunning, and now, he had been entrusted with Leofric's survival.

Every morning, Leofric would rise before the sun, forced to leave the warmth of the small fire near the barracks. His breath would fog in the bitter air as he followed Rodrigo to the training grounds.

It was a cold, open field surrounded by snow-covered trees. On those mornings, the sky would often be the color of slate, and the ground would crunch beneath their boots as they practiced.

Rodrigo taught Leofric how to move silently, how to strike with precision, how to read the flow of a battle. Farfel, on the other hand, had focused on brute force, believing strength was all that mattered. But Rodrigo knew better.

"Strength is nothing if you can't control it," he would say, his accent thick but his words clear.

"The mind must guide the body."

Leofric was forced to relearn everything. His arms, once stiff from endless hours of labor, began to loosen, his movements more fluid. The rhythm of combat started to feel natural to him, as though it had always been a part of him, buried deep beneath the weight of his captivity.

The Spaniard also taught him something far more subtle, how to read a man's face, how to understand his intentions before he ever drew his sword.

"The eyes are the windows to the soul," Rodrigo would whisper.

"See the lies before they leave his lips."

Despite his kindness, Rodrigo was no fool. He understood the Viking mentality all too well, and he knew how to survive in this hostile environment. He had come to the northern lands as part of a larger group of mercenaries, but had since learned that aligning himself with Farfel's army was the key to his survival. But this didn't mean he sympathized with Farfel's methods. If anything, he had a quiet resentment for the brutality that ruled this land.

There were nights when Leofric would wake from nightmares, drenched in sweat, visions of his homeland in flames.

It was on one such night that Rodrigo found him in the cold, sitting alone near the fire.

"Nightmares?" Rodrigo's voice was low, but there was a trace of concern.

Leofric nodded, unable to speak. The images of his family's destruction haunted him still. Rodrigo sat beside him, his cloak heavy with frost.

"You'll never forget them," he said.

"But the past is a weight. You must learn to carry it, not let it crush you."

The words resonated with Leofric, though he could not fully understand their meaning yet. His heart ached for the people he had lost, for the life that had been ripped from him. But with every day that passed, he began to feel something more powerful than the grief, the fire of survival.

As winter dragged on, the Viking camp grew accustomed to the changing dynamics. Leofric's skill in combat improved, his agility in battle something that even the most hardened warriors noticed. And Farfel, though silent, could not help but take some pride in Leofric's progress, even if he never voiced it.

Leofric's thoughts began to wander to other things during the long nights of training. He had seen the longships that brought the Viking horde, their sails dark against the gray sky, their hulls slicing through the icy waters. These were not mere raiders. They were conquerors, a force that dominated the seas and left terror in their wake.

But now, in this bleak wilderness, as the days shortened and the nights stretched on forever, Leofric found something else, a drive that had not existed before. Survival was no longer just a way to escape death; it was something to be mastered, to be controlled. And through that mastery, perhaps he could return to his people, to his homeland.

But even as he thought of home, there was an unsettling feeling growing inside him, one he could not name. Something deeper, more primal. The long winters and harsh training were changing him in ways he didn't yet understand.

Rodrigo noticed this, too.

"You are a long way from home, Leofric," he would say, his voice carrying a hint of something darker.

"But the road you walk now... it will shape you into something different. Be careful."

Leofric didn't know it then, but the journey that had begun with a Viking horde and a forced life of servitude was far from over. It had only just begun to reveal its true purpose, and in time, he would understand what he had become.

The sound of the longships cutting through the waves was a familiar one, yet Leofric's heart drummed louder than the rhythm of the oars beneath him. The scent of salt and seaweed filled the air as they approached Lindisfarne. He had not set foot on this island since his capture, three years earlier, when the Viking horde had taken everything from him. The faces of his family haunted his thoughts, but none more so than his father.

Why didn't he save me? The question gnawed at him with a hunger that only grew as the island grew larger on the horizon.

Lindisfarne, his home, or what was left of it, was just as he remembered: the rolling hills, the distant cliffs, and the village nestled between them. Yet there was a cold emptiness in the air that felt different now. It was a bitter reminder of all he had lost.

His hands tightened around the hilt of his sword as the

ship glided to shore. The warriors in Farfel's horde cheered, eager for the pillage to begin, but Leofric's mind was elsewhere. He had come back for something far more personal. This wasn't just another raid. This was vengeance.

Farfel's orders were clear, sack the village, take what they could, and burn the rest. But for Leofric, this was a reckoning. His feet hit the muddy shore, and the sounds of the Viking horde following him felt distant, almost muffled. In that moment, all that mattered was the one man who had failed him.

As they stormed through the village, Leofric's gaze swept across the homes, the familiar sights of his childhood. It wasn't the village that mattered, though, it was the man who had once called himself his father.

The memories of his father's proud stance, his booming voice, and his heavy hand made Leofric's blood burn with rage.

Where was he? Why hadn't he come for me?

Leofric spotted the figure in the center of the village.

His father, older now, with a graying beard and weathered face, was standing there, rallying the villagers, trying to defend them against the inevitable onslaught. Leofric's heart pounded in his chest. He couldn't stop himself, couldn't control the fury building inside him.

He pushed through the ranks of the Viking raiders, his body moving as if it were driven by something primal. His father turned at the sound of Leofric's footsteps, his eyes wide with recognition.

"You," the older man said.

His voice wavered as he reached for his axe.

"Leofric…"

It was all the invitation Leofric needed. He didn't hesitate.

His sword flashed through the air, and with a sickening thud, it cleaved through his father's chest, sending the older man to the ground in a spray of blood. His father's eyes widened in disbelief, but Leofric didn't feel a shred of remorse. He had been waiting for this moment, and now that it was here, it was almost too easy. Too clean.

"*Why?*" his father gasped, his breath a ragged wheeze.

"*Why would you…*"

Leofric's voice was cold, devoid of any compassion.

"You didn't come for me. You left me to die."

And with that, he turned away, leaving his father's blood to stain the earth. The screams of the villagers faded into the background as Leofric's mind spun. He didn't know if he felt liberated or hollow. There was no closure in killing the man who had once been his protector. Only emptiness.

The Viking horde, in the meantime, continued its raid. The village fell quickly to the might of the Vikings. The air was thick with the smoke of burning homes, the cries of the innocent, and the guttural sounds of warriors claiming their spoils.

But there was another target that Leofric had in mind, the monastery, just beyond the village. The monks there had been of no consequence to him in his past life, but now, they were the key to something else. They had knowledge, and perhaps one of them would lead him to the answers he sought.

The monks put up a desperate, though futile, defense as the Vikings stormed through the gates. They're gold, scrolls and sacred items were no longer protected.

Leofric hacked his way through the cloisters, the scent of incense mixing with blood as the monastery fell into chaos. He moved swiftly, carving through the defenseless men, his mind fixated on one thing:

Where is Godwulf?

Amid the carnage, Leofric's eyes caught a monk, young, perhaps a student. His robes were stained with the blood of his brethren, but there was something different about him. His face was calm, almost serene, despite the violence around him.

Leofric approached, sword in hand, and grabbed the monk by the collar, pulling him to his feet.

"You will help me find Godwulf," he growled, his voice low and threatening. The monk didn't flinch.

"I... I do not know who you speak of," the monk stammered, his voice trembling.

Leofric's grip tightened.

"You will know soon enough."

Just then, a flash of movement caught his eye, an outsider, a figure moving swiftly through the smoke and chaos. It was Komo, the warrior who had once been a part of Farfel's army, now fleeing the carnage, likely trying to escape before the raid reached its peak. Komo had been close to Godwulf before, had known his story, his clan.

Leofric hesitated for only a moment, then shoved the monk aside and pursued Komo. The fleeing monk was fast, but Leofric was faster, his rage propelling him through the monastery like a force of nature. He reached the edge of the courtyard just in time to see Komo slip through the back gate, disappearing into the wilderness beyond.

Leofric cursed under his breath. But he didn't stop. This was the only lead he had, the only chance to find the answers he craved.

The monk, still on the ground, looked up in fear.

"Please, I—"

Leofric's eyes darkened.

"You will be useful," he said coldly, dragging the monk to his feet.

"You'll come with me. Perhaps you know more than you think."

As he led the monk away from the destruction, Leofric's thoughts were a whirlwind of fury. His past had been violently torn apart, and now the pieces were scattered across the world, from his family's ruin to the whispers of Godwulf's name.

He could almost feel the weight of destiny upon him. What had been a quest for vengeance had now become something else, something darker, more dangerous. And as they began their journey, Leofric could only wonder:

What path will this take me down?

JOHN J WISELEY

THE CAVE

After a tense ride, Komo dismounts and runs to find his pupil. Komo's breath came in heavy gasps as he climbed the rocky path leading up to the cave. The wind had picked up, howling across the craggy hills, but he pushed forward, his mind racing. The raid on Lindisfarne had left him unsettled, his thoughts tangled with the memories of the other monks.

The cold was biting, but it wasn't the chill of the mountain air that made Komo's spine prickle with unease, it was the sense that he was walking into something he couldn't fully understand. Something had changed in the winds of fate, something dark and powerful. Leofric was a man on the edge of something terrible, and Komo knew he had to speak to Godwulf before it was too late.

When the entrance to the cave came into view, Komo's heart eased, if only for a moment. The towering rocks loomed above him, casting long shadows that seemed to draw him in like an old friend. The cave was a place of power, a sanctuary for those who sought refuge from the world outside.

Komo entered the cave, his footsteps echoing off the stone walls. The dim light of the flickering torches revealed the figure of Godwulf, sitting in meditation. His cloak was draped around him, the faint glow of the fire casting long shadows across his face. His eyes were closed, but Komo knew he was aware of his presence.

He approached slowly, careful not to disrupt Godwulf's concentration. But even as he neared, he could sense that something had changed in the air, something that made the hairs on his neck stand on end.

"Godwulf," Komo said softly, breaking the silence.

"There was another raid."

Godwulf opened his eyes, their golden hue flickering like embers in the darkness. There was a calmness in his gaze, but beneath it, a sharp intelligence burned, something ancient, something not entirely human.

"What happened?" Godwulf's voice was calm, yet carried a weight to it, as if the very air around him shifted with his words.

"The village and the monastery were attacked. Many people died. I fled. Your brother took part in the attack."

Godwulf stood, his long cloak flowing like a shadow behind him. He paced slowly, his mind processing Komo's words with a quiet intensity. He had anticipated this moment, had known that the forces at play were greater than even his own understanding. But he could not let his focus falter now.

"I have seen it in the winds," Godwulf said, his voice low and steady.

"Leofric is not just a man anymore. He is becoming something else. He was always a warrior at heart, but now, his thirst for vengeance is driving him down a darker path. His rage will consume him, Komo. It already has, and he doesn't even know it."

Komo could see that Godwulf had matured immensely in

such a short time and he was very proud.

"Leofric's path is his own to walk. But I must prepare for what is to come. I have made great strides in my training with the dragons. They have shown me their secrets, their ancient ways. I can feel the power of their blood coursing through me, strengthening my connection to the Draco Supreme."

Komo's eyes widened.

"The Draco Supreme? You've made contact with him?"

Godwulf nodded slowly.

"I have. The dragons are not mere beasts. They are the keepers of the world's oldest knowledge. They have seen the rise and fall of empires, and they will help me unlock the secrets that will shape our future. But that power comes at a cost. There are forces at work, ones that are far beyond us. Leofric's journey is only part of the greater storm that is coming."

Komo stepped forward, his brow knitted with worry.

"You speak of a storm… but what is it you plan to do with the dragons? How will they help us against Leofric?"

Godwulf's gaze turned distant, as if his mind was already far away, tracing the currents of time and destiny.

"The dragons hold the key to unlocking not only Leofric's curse but also the very forces that govern this world. The dragon clans can bring balance to the world. They have done it before and I believe it is time for them to do it again. My connection with them is growing stronger every day. Soon, I will have the power to confront the greatest threats, Leofric, the horde, and any who seek to destroy humanity."

Godwulf turned to him, his eyes glowing with an eerie

determination. "We need to prepare. The dragons will help us, but it is up to us to forge the path forward. I will arrange a meeting with my brother, to try and understand him. I fear that it will be in vain, but I will try to bring peace to his heart."

Komo nodded slowly, the weight of their mission settling on his shoulders. As much as he feared the coming storm, he knew there was no turning back now. The future was in their hands, and whatever happened, they had to see it through.

With one last glance at the mountain peaks beyond, Godwulf turned toward the shadows of his cave, his mind already focused on the ancient creatures who would shape their destiny. And Komo, despite the unease that lingered, knew they had no choice but to walk this dangerous path together.

THE MEETING

The journey from Lindisfarne to Norway had been long and arduous. Leofric, still burdened with the weight of his father's death, had kept his focus on the task ahead, finding Godwulf, confronting him, and learning the truth of his brother's involvement in all of this. It wasn't enough that he had killed his father, though. No, that wasn't the full measure of his vengeance. He needed answers, and he was certain Godwulf held the key to it all.

Angus, the young monk who had been taken hostage during the raid, was of use when it came to tracking down Godwulf. But there was something strange about the monk, his eyes were deep, full of secrets, and in their strange, quiet moments, he had begun speaking of things that made Leofric uneasy.

The monk spoke with a calm assurance, his voice echoing in Leofric's mind rather than through his lips.

Godwulf, the one you seek, is not far.

Leofric had barely noticed the moment when Angus had shifted from speaking aloud to speaking telepathically.

He wasn't sure if it was a trick or if something more powerful was at play. But the words came clearer each time, and Leofric began to realize that his prisoner might be far more involved in the game than he had initially thought.

The monk guided them through the frozen mountains of Norway, across the treacherous terrain that Leofric had once known like the back of his hand. But something in the monk's presence unnerved him now. It was as though the very earth seemed to hum with the monk's whispers. It wasn't long before they reached a hidden clearing in the mountains, a place where the earth felt strangely alive, and the trees bowed their boughs low, as if paying homage to something ancient.

Angus spoke, his voice echoing in Leofric's mind once more.

We have arranged the meeting, Leofric. Godwulf will be here. But you must understand, there are things greater than either of you.

Leofric glanced at the monk.

"I don't care about greater things. I care about seeing my brother."

Angus nodded as if he already knew.

Then you shall have him. But be warned—he does not come alone.

Leofric gripped the hilt of his sword tightly, the cold wind biting into his skin. His breath came in sharp, uneven puffs as he waited. His pulse quickened. He had come for Godwulf. He had come for answers. And he would not be denied.

The silence in the clearing grew unbearable until the earth seemed to shudder beneath their feet. Suddenly, a figure appeared on the horizon, a silhouette against the dim light of the setting sun. Leofric's heart skipped a beat. His brother, Godwulf, was here.

But something else followed in Godwulf's wake, a massive shadow that loomed larger as it drew near.

Leofric's eyes widened. He had heard stories of creatures such as these, ancient and fearsome, beasts that no man could hope to tame. It was Hycrest, the dragon, its massive wings folding against its back as it landed with a thunderous crash. Its scales shimmered in the twilight, a shifting mix of greens and golds, its eyes gleaming with an intelligence that could only be described as ancient.

Godwulf approached, his face as serene and unreadable as ever, his eyes meeting Leofric's with a quiet sadness. There was no warmth in their greeting, only an understanding that ran deep beneath the surface.

"Leofric," Godwulf said softly.

"You've come."

Leofric sneered, his anger bubbling to the surface.

"I've come for answers. And for you. You've always been the one to walk away, to hide in the shadows, while I fought for survival. You should have saved me. You should have come back for me."

Godwulf didn't flinch.

"I could not, brother. There were things, forces beyond us, that kept me from you. But I have never forgotten you."

Leofric's fists clenched. The rage inside him threatened to break free, and his voice hardened as he spat out the words.

"I killed our father, Godwulf. I killed him, and I don't regret it.

The words hung in the air between them, heavy with the weight of years of silence and betrayal. Godwulf's expression faltered, the briefest flicker of pain flashing in his eyes.

But it was gone before Leofric could fully grasp it. Instead, his brother's gaze turned steady, calm, though there was something like sorrow there. Godwulf loved his father dearly, but he remained calm.

"I never wanted you to suffer, Leofric," Godwulf said.

"But we are bound by a fate we do not control."

At that moment, the ground seemed to tremble again, and Hycrest, standing tall beside Godwulf, unfurled its massive wings. The dragon's fiery breath blasted the air around them, the heat radiating in waves. Leofric stumbled back, feeling the burn of the air on his face.

Hycrest's eyes blazed with warning, and the great beast gave a low growl, smoke rising from its nostrils. Leofric's gaze locked onto Godwulf.

"This creature will not stop me. Nothing will. The next time we meet, I will kill you, brother. You and your dragon."

Godwulf's eyes flickered with something, was it regret? He placed a hand on the great dragon's side, his fingers brushing the ancient scales with a reverence that almost seemed to transmit through the air itself.

"Then I will prepare for it," Godwulf replied, his voice steady but laced with the weight of an impending storm.

"We will face what comes, Leofric. But you do not yet understand what you are up against."

Leofric stood tall, his sword still gripped tightly in his hand, his breath coming in ragged gasps from the heated air. He did not back down.

"Next time," Leofric snarled, "you'll regret letting me live."

With that, Leofric turned on his heel, leaving the clearing and heading toward the mountains once more, the weight of his brother's silence burning into his soul. The echoes of Hycrest's growl and the steady footsteps of Godwulf haunted him, but it didn't matter. He would find a way to defeat them. He had to.

THE GREAT FALL

The journey to find the Draco Supreme was treacherous, but Leofric was relentless. Angus, the monk, had proven his worth, guiding him through the frozen wastelands and jagged mountain passes of Norway with an unnatural sense of direction. Though Leofric still didn't fully trust him, he needed the monk's strange powers, his ability to sense things unseen, to reach out with his mind and find those who did not wish to be found.

For weeks, they traveled deeper into the wilds, following cryptic whispers and long-forgotten trails. They crossed frozen rivers, scaled sheer cliffs, and traversed dark caves where even the bravest warriors feared to tread. Leofric felt something growing inside him during the journey, a dark hunger, an insatiable thirst for power. He had stood before Godwulf and his dragon and felt powerless. That would not happen again.

Then, one day, Angus stopped. They had reached a desolate valley, shrouded in mist and silence. At its heart, half-buried in the ice and stone, was the entrance to a cavern unlike any they had seen before.

The mouth of the cave gaped open like the maw of some ancient beast, its walls lined with jagged black rock, pulsing faintly with a dim, otherworldly glow.

"This is the place," Angus whispered.

Leofric stepped forward, gripping his sword as they descended into the darkness. The air grew thick, almost alive, pressing against them with a weight that made it difficult to breathe. A heavy presence filled the cavern, something ancient, something watching. Then, at the very heart of the cave, they found it.

The Draco Supreme.

The creature lay curled on a massive stone dais, its scales blackened and dull with age. Unlike the other dragons Leofric had seen, this one had no wings, its massive body coiled like a serpent, its head crowned with twisting, jagged horns. Its golden eyes opened as they approached, filled with a wisdom and exhaustion that spoke of countless centuries.

Leofric took a cautious step forward, his breath shallow. This was the being that had granted Godwulf his power, the one who had connected him to the dragons. If the Draco Supreme was destroyed, Godwulf would be severed from the dragon clans, left alone without their guidance.

The great beast exhaled slowly, its voice not spoken aloud but instead echoing in their minds.

"You come seeking power… but you do not understand the forces at play."

Leofric tightened his grip on his sword.

"I don't need to understand. I need to destroy you."

The Draco Supreme's gaze flickered to Angus. The monk bowed his head, his hands trembling as if struggling against something unseen. The ancient dragon let out a low rumble, something between a sigh and a growl.

"Your path is shrouded in darkness, Leofric of the North. You believe that slaying me will make you victorious. But you do not yet know what you have become."

Leofric sneered.

"Enough riddles."

With a swift motion, he drove his sword forward. The blade struck true, piercing through the ancient scales.

The Draco Supreme let out a low, throaty sound, not quite pain, but a sigh of inevitability. As the life faded from its golden eyes, it released one final thought.

A message. A message meant only for Godwulf. **Far away, in his mountain refuge, Godwulf stiffened.** The moment was brief but overwhelming. A voice boomed in his mind, the last whisper of something ancient and irreplaceable.

"The storm comes. The blood of the brothers shall decide the fate of the dragons."

Then, silence. A void. Godwulf staggered, gripping the rocky walls of his cave as Hycrest, his dragon companion, lifted his great head in sudden awareness. The connection was gone. The Draco Supreme was dead.

Godwulf clenched his fists. His brother had done this. But Leofric had miscalculated. The Draco Supreme had once been the bridge between the dragon clans and the world of men. He had been the voice that connected them, the link that allowed communication. But Godwulf had grown beyond that. His own power had grown strong enough to connect directly with the dragons.

His mind reached out, stretching across vast distances, and one by one, he felt them.

Dragons, great and small. They heard him. They answered. Leofric thought he had severed Godwulf's power. He had only made him stronger.

A CALL TO ARMS

The hall was thick with the scent of mead, sweat, and burning tallow. Warriors feasted and drank loudly, their voices rising in laughter and song, oblivious to the storm that brewed in their midst. At the head of the great longhouse sat Farfel, his massive frame draped in furs, his beard thick and wild as ever. The warlord had grown stronger, his influence stretching across the fjords, his warriors numbering in the thousands. But Leofric knew, Farfel was always hungry for more.

Leofric approached the high table with slow, deliberate steps. He had spent years fighting at Farfel's side, enduring his cruelty, proving himself worthy. But now, he needed something far greater than survival. He needed war.

Farfel eyed him with suspicion.

"You come back from your hunt empty-handed, Leofric?" He smirked.

"Or did you finally learn that some beasts cannot be tamed?"

Leofric knelt slightly, a mock show of respect.

"I bring news, not trophies. A prize greater than gold,

greater than slaves."

He let his words sink in before continuing.

"I know where the dragons nest. I know where my brother hides. And I know how to end them both."

The room fell silent. Warriors turned, their ears catching only one word, **dragons.**

Farfel leaned forward, interest flickering in his dark eyes.

"Speak."

Leofric stepped closer.

"My brother Godwulf has gathered the dragon clans on the shores near his mountain caves. They prepare for war, but they are not ready. Not yet. If we strike now, before they organize, we can burn them from the sky."

Murmurs spread through the hall. Some men looked fearful, others intrigued. Farfel studied Leofric carefully.

"And how do you know this?"

Leofric's lip curled.

"Because I killed the Draco Supreme."

The hall erupted. Some warriors cursed, others cheered. Farfel's expression darkened with intrigue.

"You killed the one who spoke for the dragons?"

Leofric nodded.

"And without their ancient leader, the dragons are leaderless. My brother will try to command them, but we both know he is no warlord. He is weak. If we strike first, if we hit them hard, we will wipe out the dragon clans before they can unite under him."

Farfel stroked his beard, eyes gleaming with greed.

"Dragons," he muttered.

"A true challenge. A fight worthy of a warrior's saga."

He turned to his men.

"Would you fight beside me to claim the greatest glory known to man? Would you march with me to slay the beasts of legend?"

A roar erupted from the hall. Leofric smiled. The viking war had begun.

The wind howled along the shoreline, whipping salt and sand into the air. The beach stretched wide beneath the looming cliffs of the dragon caves, and upon it stood Godwulf, his face turned toward the sky. The air vibrated with power, not from the earth, but from the massive creatures that landed in waves.

They came from all corners of the land. The great red dragons of the eastern mountains, their scales shimmering like molten rock. The slender blue serpents of the fjords, their eyes sharp and cold as the sea. The black-winged beasts of the northern tundra, their breath thick with frost. They landed in formations, warriors of the sky, each more fearsome than the last.

Godwulf stood among them, his hand resting on Hycrest's massive neck. He did not need the Draco Supreme to reach them now. His mind had stretched beyond what he had ever imagined, his thoughts connecting like a web to every dragon in the land.

They come for us, he told them, his voice echoing in their minds. **A horde of men, led by my brother. They will come with**

fire, with steel, with hatred in their hearts. They seek to end you.

The dragons rumbled in response, wings flaring, tails lashing against the sand.

We do not fear men, one of the elder dragons growled, a massive beast with scales as white as snow.

No, Godwulf answered. **But you must respect them. They will not fight like before. They have learned our ways, our weaknesses. They will not flee. They will not break. They come with one goal—to wipe you out.**

A deep silence followed. Then, Hycrest stepped forward.

Then we will show them why the sky belongs to us.

A chorus of roars shook the cliffs, sending avalanches of stone tumbling into the sea. The dragons, once scattered and divided, now stood as one.

Godwulf turned toward the horizon. His brother was coming. The dragon war had begun.

THE WAR FLEET

The longhouses of the fjord were alive with the clamor of war. Blacksmiths pounded glowing metal into swords and axes, their rhythmic hammering echoing across the valley. Women and thralls rushed to and from the docks, carrying bundles of dried meat, barrels of water, and crates of arrows. The scent of pitch and tar filled the air as men sealed the hulls of the longships, ensuring they would endure the grueling journey ahead.

Leofric stood atop a rocky outcrop overlooking the harbor, watching the chaos unfold. Below him, dozens of longships bobbed in the cold waters, their dragon-headed prows snarling toward the sea. Each ship held warriors, seasoned raiders, young berserkers eager for glory, and veterans who had bled for Farfel time and time again. The warlord himself stood on the docks, barking orders, his thick arms crossed as he inspected the preparations.

Leofric strode down to meet him.

"We sail at dawn?"

Farfel smirked, his eyes glinting with savage excitement.

"We sail when the tide is high, and the gods demand blood." He gestured to the ships.

"The men are ready. The winds favor us. When we land, we strike hard. No hesitation. No mercy."

Leofric nodded.

"Good. Godwulf will be expecting us, but he does not know when. If we strike before his dragons are fully united, we can break him."

Farfel's grin widened.

"You want your brother dead that badly?"

Leofric's expression darkened.

"I want him broken. I want him to watch as everything he loves burns."

Farfel clapped him on the shoulder.

"Then you will have your war."

By nightfall, the warriors gathered at the shore, forming ranks in front of their respective longships. The warbands were divided, each led by seasoned jarls who had plundered a hundred shores. The largest ship, Farfel's own, bore black sails adorned with the sigil of a crimson wolf.

Leofric's ship, smaller but fast, carried the sigil of a serpent wrapped around a broken sword—a new mark he had claimed as his own.

A fire was lit on the highest hill, and the war horns sounded. One by one, the warriors boarded their ships, their weapons clanking, their voices raised in chants of battle and death. The air was thick with tension, but also with something else, eagerness. Bloodlust.

As the tide swelled, the longships were pushed into the water, oars dipping into the waves in perfect unison. The wind caught the sails, and the fleet lurched forward, slicing through the black sea. The journey had begun.

For days, the ships cut through the endless ocean. The warriors sang to the waves, their voices rising over the roar of the wind. The gods of war were invoked with each song, offerings of mead poured into the sea in hopes of a glorious battle. The waters were rough, the skies unforgiving, but the fleet pressed on, their course set for the dragon-haunted shores where Godwulf waited.

Leofric stood at the prow of his ship, eyes fixed on the distant horizon.

His fingers traced the hilt of his sword. He could feel it, his brother knew he was coming. He welcomed it.

One night, as the sea churned beneath them and the moon cast a silver path across the waves, Farfel called a war council on his ship. The leaders of the raiding parties gathered in a tight circle, the only light coming from a small iron lantern.

"Godwulf will have defenses," Farfel growled.

"Not just dragons, but men who follow him. We need to strike fast, hit the caves before they have time to organize. Fire will be our best weapon. Burn the fields, the cliffs, the nests. Let them choke on smoke before they ever take to the sky."

Leofric leaned forward.

"And if the dragons rise against us?"

Farfel grinned.

"Then we give them a death worthy of a saga."

Laughter followed, though beneath it, there was unease. No matter how fierce these warriors were, they were marching into battle against creatures of legend.

The next day, the winds changed. A storm brewed on the horizon, dark clouds rolling in like an omen. Leofric took it as a sign, the gods were watching. Their war was coming.

Far away, on the misty shores where dragons gathered, Godwulf sat in quiet meditation.

The cave was dim, illuminated only by the soft glow of the embers in the firepit. Komo sat beside him, cross-legged, his eyes closed, his breath slow and measured. The old mystic had not spoken much since returning from his doomed escape at Lindisfarne. He had simply followed Godwulf into the mountains, as if knowing this moment would come.

"They are coming," Godwulf murmured.

Komo's eyes remained shut.

"Yes."

Godwulf exhaled slowly, reaching out with his mind. He did not need scouts to tell him what he already knew. He could feel Leofric's presence across the vast distance, burning with hatred, moving steadily toward him like a blade drawn for war.

But Godwulf did not fear him.

He opened his mind further. The dragons. He could feel them, all of them, great and small, their minds connected to his own. Some burned with fury, others with caution, but they were all waiting for his command.

"We will not attack first," he said at last.

Komo finally opened his eyes.

"You would let the war come to us?"

Godwulf nodded.

"They will come with arrogance. They will come believing they can slaughter the dragon clans like cattle. But we have the land, the sky, and the fire of the ancients on our side."

Komo studied him for a long moment.

"You have become something more than a man, Godwulf."

Godwulf met his gaze.

"Then it is time for my brother to see it."

Outside, the wind howled across the cliffs, carrying the scent of salt and war. The dragons stirred. Their wings stretched in the moonlight. The battle was near.

THE BROTHERS' FELSPAR

The longships cut through the dark waters like knives, their dragon-headed prows slicing the waves as they neared the mist-covered shore. The rhythmic beat of war drums echoed across the sea, a deep and steady pulse that matched the pounding hearts of the warriors aboard.

Leofric stood at the prow of his ship, eyes narrowed as he tried to pierce through the thickening mist. It curled around them like ghostly fingers, hiding the land ahead. The beach should have been in sight by now, but all he saw was endless fog.

Then, a shape emerged. At first, it looked like another longship, a massive one, with a dragon's head more fearsome than any carved prow he had ever seen. The mist slithered around its form, revealing gleaming scales like black iron, a body long and coiled, half-submerged in the water.

Leofric's blood turned to ice. It was no ship. It was a dragon. A monstrous beast, its yellow eyes glowing like lanterns in the fog.

The warriors on the lead ship froze, their hands tightening around swords and axes. Some gasped in awe, others whispered prayers to their gods.

Then the dragon opened its maw. A torrent of fire erupted from its throat, roaring like an inferno. It washed over the ship in an instant, turning wood, sail, and men into an explosion of flames. The screams of the dying were drowned by the crackling of burning timber. The fire devoured everything, and in seconds, the ship was nothing but a charred husk sinking into the sea. Panic rippled through the fleet.

"ROW FASTER!" Farfel bellowed from his own ship.

"TO THE SHORE! MOVE!"

The dragon did not linger. It slithered back into the mist, vanishing like a phantom. But before the warriors could regain their composure, it struck again. Another ship erupted into flames. Then another.

The dragon soared from the water, its massive wings sending waves crashing against the remaining longships. It flew toward the towering cliffs, where shadows waited above.

Leofric cursed under his breath. He knew what was coming next. The real battle had not yet begun.

The survivors rowed furiously, their ships scraping against the rocky shore. As soon as the keels hit land, warriors leapt into the shallows, dragging themselves onto the beach. Smoke billowed from the wreckage behind them, lighting the sky with an eerie orange glow.

Farfel wasted no time. He barked orders, rallying his men. "Form ranks! Shields up! We take the cliffs now!"

Leofric stood at his side, scanning the steep incline before them. The grassy hill stretched upward, leading to the plateau above. And there, silhouetted against the stormy sky, stood their enemy.

Godwulf. And twenty-two dragons.

The sight of them made Leofric's pulse quicken. He had expected resistance, but this, this was something else. He had killed the Draco Supreme. The dragons should have been leaderless, scattered. How had they united? His fists clenched. He would find out soon enough.

Farfel raised his axe.

"MOVE!"

The horde of Northmen surged forward, boots pounding against the earth. The climb was steep, the hill sapping their energy with each step. The weight of their weapons and armor dragged at them, their breaths growing heavier.

Leofric ran among them, his mind clouded with rage. Godwulf stood motionless at the top, clad in a simple brown robe, watching as if he already knew the outcome.

Angus, the monk, struggled to keep up, his robes soaked in sweat, his breathing ragged. He had done his part, guiding Leofric to the Draco Supreme's lair. But now, he was a reminder of something Leofric did not want to acknowledge, his failure to break Godwulf before this moment.

With a snarl, Leofric stopped running and grabbed Angus by the collar and dragged him forward.

"What do you see?" he demanded.

Angus gasped, his eyes darting up at the dragons.

"It's over, Leofric. You don't understand—"

Leofric didn't let him finish. He drove his sword into the

monk's chest, twisting it as Angus choked on his last breath. Blood spattered across Leofric's armor as he let the body fall.

"I understand enough."

The Vikings finally reached the plateau. And there, the war truly began. The moment the first Northman stepped onto the field, the dragons attacked.

With a deafening roar, the beasts took to the sky, their wings sending gusts of wind that knocked warriors off their feet. Fire rained down upon them, setting shields and flesh ablaze. The air filled with the smell of burning hair, melting armor, and the screams of dying men.

Farfel swung his axe at a diving dragon, but the beast was too fast, its tail whipping through the ranks and sending warriors tumbling. Another dragon spewed a jet of ice, freezing a dozen men in place before shattering them with a swipe of its claws.

Leofric fought with savage fury, cutting down any dragon that came too close. He ducked under a massive wing, driving his sword into the belly of a smaller beast.

The dragon screeched, but before Leofric could finish it, another came down upon him, nearly crushing him beneath its weight. Through the chaos, he locked eyes with Godwulf.

His brother stood in the center of it all, untouched, unmoved. His presence radiated power. The dragons were not fighting blindly, they were fighting as one. And Leofric finally understood.

Godwulf had not needed the Draco Supreme. He had become what the Supreme once was. Fury boiled inside Leofric. He let out a battle cry and charged. Godwulf raised a hand.

Hycrest, the acid breather, swiftly landed between them, its fangs bared. It reared its head, prepared to unleash a torrent of fire.

Leofric skidded to a halt.

The war raged on around them. Vikings screamed, dragons roared, steel clashed, fire consumed the field. And for the first time in his life, Leofric knew fear.

THE FATED DUO

Leofric stood frozen, his sword heavy in his grip. The dragon before him, a massive, ancient beast with emerald scales and golden eyes, blocked his path to Godwulf. Smoke and flame swirled around them, and the battlefield was thick with the stench of burning flesh. His ears rang with the screams of dying men and the roars of the dragons, but through it all, one undeniable truth settled in his mind.

They were losing.

The Northmen were dying faster than they could fight. The dragons were too powerful, too many. He could see it in the weary eyes of Farfel, who swung his axe at a diving beast, only to be swept away like a child's toy. He could see it in the scattered, broken shield wall, now more bodies than warriors.

And he could see it in his own fate. This was his end. He had led his people to their doom. But if he was going to die, he would not do so without taking something from his brother.

His eyes flicked toward Komo, standing at Godwulf's side.

The wise monk had been with his brother since the beginning, guiding him, shaping him. If Leofric could not kill Godwulf, he could still wound him.

His hand moved quickly, snatching the bow from his back. His fingers found the arrow and notched it in one smooth motion. Godwulf had barely realized what was happening when Leofric loosed the shot.

The arrow cut through the air, striking deep into Komo's chest.

Komo gasped, stumbling backward, his aged fingers grasping at the shaft. Blood bloomed across his robes as he collapsed.

"No!"

Godwulf's voice tore through the battlefield like a storm. Leofric smirked. He had finally hurt him. Then, the sky darkened. Godwulf's eyes burned with fury. His body tensed, but he did not move toward Leofric.

Instead, he turned to Hycrest. The great dragon let out a slow, deep growl, its golden eyes narrowing on Leofric.

"Do it," Godwulf commanded.

Hycrest reared back, his chest swelling as a sickly green light pulsed from deep within. Then, with a guttural roar, the dragon spewed forth a torrent of acidic bile.

Leofric barely had time to react before the liquid fire engulfed him. Pain. More pain than he had ever known. The acid ate through his armor, his flesh, his very bones. He screamed, but his voice broke into a choking gurgle as his throat melted. His hands clawed at his own skin, his body convulsing as the acid consumed him inch by inch. The world blurred. His vision darkened. He had led his people to their doom. And now, he was paying the price.

The war was over. The few remaining Vikings, those who had not been crushed, burned, or frozen by the dragons, saw the fate of their leader and knew they had no hope. They ran. Some toward the sea, others into the forests beyond the cliffs, but they were only a handful. Their great army was no more. The dragons did not pursue. There was no need.

One by one, the mighty beasts took to the skies, gathering the dead Northmen in their claws and carrying them to the sea. The tide had long since put out the flames of the ruined ships, leaving the broken wreckage to crash aimlessly against the rocky shore.

The bodies were dropped into the cold waters, sinking into the depths, lost to time. The Vikings had come in fire and fury. And they had been washed away.

Godwulf knelt beside Komo, cradling his mentor's head. Komo's breath was shallow, his life slipping away.

"You have done well," Komo whispered, his voice barely audible.

"The balance is restored."

Godwulf's jaw tightened.

"Stay with me."

Komo gave a weak smile.

"My time was always meant to end here."

His eyes fluttered closed. "Be at peace, Godwulf."

With that, Komo exhaled his final breath.

Godwulf closed his mentor's eyes and placed a hand over his

chest. Then, he turned to the cliffs, where the dragons had begun to disperse.

Hycrest stood beside him, gazing out over the now-quiet battlefield. The silence was deafening.

"The war is done," Godwulf murmured.

Hycrest rumbled in agreement.

"What will become of the dragons now?"

Godwulf asked.

The great dragon lifted his head, staring toward the horizon.

"They will return when they are needed."

Then, with a mighty leap, Hycrest took to the sky, his wings carrying him into the clouds. One by one, the dragons followed, their forms vanishing into the heavens.

Godwulf remained on the beach, the waves lapping at the shore, the wind carrying away the last echoes of battle. He sat in meditation, the weight of everything settling upon him. For now, there was peace.

And for the first time in a long while, the world was quiet.

The End

Made in the USA
Columbia, SC
06 March 2025